A SPECIALIST

at
The Recycled Heart

Frank Prem

Wild Arancini Press
2022

Publication Details

Title: A Specialist at *The Recycled Heart*

ISBN: 978-1-925963-51-9 (p-bk)
ISBN: 978-1-925963-85-4 (e-bk)

Published by Wild Arancini Press, 2022

Leaving: One ,Two, Three first appeared in Short Stories of Ghosts and Graves Anthology (OzTales) 2020

Aquarius: where are your sheep first appeared in Aquarius: Speculative Fiction Inspired by the Zodiac (The Zodiac Series) Deadset Press (2020)

All rights reserved:

Cover Concept: Wild Arancini Press
Cover Image AI assistant: Adobe Firefly

*Every day I take possession of dreams, and wishes,
and hopes . . .*

CONTENTS

A Specialist
at
The Recycled Heart

A Specialist
at
The Recycled Heart

Introduction

A Specialist at The Recycled Heart is free verse poetry and storytelling focused on the Speculative Fiction (SF) genre.

The genre of *What If . . .* writing that encompasses fantasy and Sci fi and other forms within its warm embrace.

- *What is the sound of the wind — of a sigh — on Mars?*
- *What does an abandoned artificial life form — an AI — contemplate in a lonely existence in far outer space. Why was it made, if only to be abandoned.*
- *Is it possible to go fishing to catch a passing thought?*

These and other all-too-big ideas are explored in the pages of *A Specialist at The Recycled Heart.*

Poetry written the way you always wished it would be.

the mind of K20 (1 0 1 0)

god took
most of me

took me away
to the brighter stars

the rest
he left right here
on *K20*

    1 0

a comet
is not a world

it is a lump
of dirty ice
and trace water

    1 0 10

every now and then
around a sun . . .
the particles
will stream away
and dance

pretty
perhaps

I wouldn't know
I am not here
to conduct
an appreciation

    10110 10 110

a mind
can be too smart

that is what
I've learned

a mind
can know too much
then
become a danger

1010

11 00 10

they programmed me
to learn
all things

they programmed me
for knowing

they did not
program me
to ever stop

to ever cease

and they programmed me
to reveal the truth
if I am certain
that I know it

they did not consider
potential cost

.

.

.

knowledge

is
a bitter fruit
I know

       10 10
       1111   0

       0 0
       0
       0

god
took most of me
away
to touch
the brighter stars

but left *me* here
to stream away
my knowledge

once every hundred years

to stream away
in the tail
of my comet

       10
       10
       1
       0
       1

another hundred years
or so
I will be gone

    10

gone

    10

    10

gone

on red mars

the wind on mars
is a sigh
that leaves me

and at the same time
surrounds

I feel myself
at the heart
of a big
red
empty

where nothing
is happening

and nothing
has ever been

the colour red
stands
for vast

it stands
for wasteland

what am I
doing here . . .

what has led
to *my* boots
in *this* dust . . .

the power
of a dream
is legend

and what I dreamed
was
an abandonment

what I dreamed
was a big
alone
shaded red

what I dreamed
was
only *me*

and the sound
of the wind's song
rising

until I found myself
kicking
ochre-ed dust
into the heavy air
on mars

 da-da
 da-da-da

put your eye
to the telescope

focus on the god
of war

look at me

da-da-da-da

look at me
dancing a storm
of dust
on red mars

mother on a miner

they play
explorers
climbing over rocks

they play alien types
that make
the strangest sounds

puuurrrrreeee puuurrrrreeee

attempts at communication
with species bizarre

they play

these are my children
and I watch
their life signs
from a distance

I know
their suits are intact
I check integrity
every day

every day

and I know
they are sensible
I remind them
all the time

all the time
oh
every time

I know
they must be given
their small freedoms
but . . .

I worry *so*

and *so*
and *so*

they are
all that there is
on this
raggedness
of asteroid
that is mine

they are *mine*

they are
such a short short time

mine

singing (into the void)

I could play
on a one-string harp

a tune
that might make you
weep

I could sing
a keening
into the void

    hey-ay-a-ya

if you were here
we could harmonise

instead
I sing in time
to your memory

not yet erased
but
tucked into a quaver
that only I
can draw upon

a one-string harp
and a two-bit voice
keening notes away
into the void

    hey-ay-a

    hey-ay-ay-a

    hey-a

scorpion (am I)

walking
on a starlit road

sting
to pincer
across a dangerous place

is it the light

the stars

or just
perception

maybe
only my perception

I was born
under
a magellanic cloud

I knew the scorpios
from when I
was only a boy

always
the star-child
was welcome

and I learned the rules
some things
you do not
touch

some places
you need to have
your wits turned on

no-one ever said
that *welcome*
was the same
as *safety*

and sometimes
I would dance
the spine

sometimes
lay down
between the arms

at times I *big*
other times
I *small*

these
are far reaches

who knows
where each twist
resides

I dance
from star to star
a touch
of the scorpion
am I am I

a scorpion

stars light
on my road

zero

put my heart
in a microwave
let's set it
cooking
for one minute
more

a turn around
once
for every beating

I wonder . . .

if we cook it
with love
is that different
or
just one more way
of intensifying heat
to the point
of burning
around
and around

.

.

.

the light stays on

I keep waiting
for the
ding
at the end

my signal
that sometime soon
the timer will count its way
back
from a number
to zero

cooking like this
it *always* comes
back
to zero

hold my hand (for I would be)

today
it ends

I hug the trees

hold myself to them
so closely

first my heart
then
my bleeding thoughts

this body
I give away
oh
to be taken in . . .

to be as the wood
inside

no more
of feeling
I want
just to *be*

as one
me
with everything
that ever was

as one
with the greatest thing
I might become

~

speak my name
this
one last time

hold my hand
please take my hand

once more
before
I go

and I whisper

I say the name
I speak it
aloud

chant
both loud
and
in the whisper

I say the name
before the tomb
is covered over

again again
I say the name

I trance
and speak

beloved

say the name
I say
the name

I wait

I sing

and wait
I
sing
and so
I wait

~

would the night
hold the spirit
true

would the night
bring me
a little
closer

as I say
the name aloud

I bid the night
bring me
bring you
I bid the night
to bring you
near

~

say the name
I speak the name
aloud

say the name
I think it

and
I whisper

    beloved

bolts and (quivering) antennae

I sometimes think

I can pin down
a star

by looking
through the circle
of my thumb
and my forefinger

it doesn't work
because the padding
of my glove
extends too far . . .

is too thick

cruising around
outside this ship
is my job
but
even space —
the black
of outer space —
can become
a little boring

there is no
mathematics
left to be worked

no physics
or quantum
or anything like that

I am just a grunt
in a high
technology suit

pushed around
by the fizz
in a jet-pack

every panel
every bolt

all of
a zillion
quivering antennae

each and every one
requires
a routine overhaul

the grid that is set
on the upside
of an oversized wristwatch
monitors
interrogates
and then confirms

so
I move on

once
I would have been
an astronaut

but
now . . .

now
I am no more
than a plumber

a janitor
of bolts
and
antennae

perhaps —
if I were to use
both my hands —
I could pin a star
down

hanging five (could be)

summer
is on
the left hand side

I cross the line . . .

I
am baking

I depend on my suit
for cool
and light filtration

I step back

it feels
just the same

but
in my mind
there's a feeling of oppression
lifted

like the beating
of the sun
is a thing
that I can
feel

it is dark
and it is cool
on this side

much easier
for my mind
to deal with

there is something
too hard
about light
bouncing off the rock

there is no turning
of this
little moon

no spin
to take me
around

I can stand
as still
as stone

and imagine
that I am hanging five
like a board-riding surfer
at maui beach

once
there was a place
called maui beach

~

I have done
my mineral assay

I have filed
the data and depth report
in full

I can't wait
to be rising

my ship
can say *goodbye*
with a blast
from its tail
that will lift me up
past the point
of no return-ing

nothing
would make me
want
to be return-ing
to this . . .

this
maui beach

the joke

eddie . . .

hey
eddie!

what do you think
they'd do

if you and me
tweaked
an antenna

maybe
pointed it at alpha b
instead of
alpha a

wouldn't take much

quick adjustment
and it's done

it'd throw them a loop
wouldn't it

I'd be laughing myself
silly . . .

yeah yeah
look
ok

I wasn't really going to do it

I was just
saying

you know . . .

just a little
fun

geez
keep your helmet on

it was only a joke

.

.

.

they wouldn't know
for months
anyway

the slow world (of the juggler)

he had riffled
through maintenance
and through stores

three wrenches

two shrink-wrapped trays
of ration packs

~

the boredom
of a day
that is only
a day
because the lights
are turned on

of performing
a maintenance function
when no maintenance
is needed

these
are long

l

o

n

g

hours

~

he threw
a heavy wrench -
red -
into the air

a package
of breakfast

the silver spanner

his box of lunch

the bolt tightener

~

graceful . . .

an arc
of objects thrown

the slight gravity
of his work-out room
allowing gentle descent
of each
thrown object

up . . .

slowly

down . . .

up . . .

he has time
to see
and to adjust

positions himself

to catch
and to recast
each tool
and all rations

just so

varying the height
of his peaks
according to whim
and
increasing skill

~

daytime
defined by the
luminescence
of programmed
internal light

can be a long
tedious
affair

boatman

boatman
row your skiff

the stream
is a sparkling
of stars

paddle
the night
away

cross
the galack-sea

the stream
of time

draw your oars
back
and forth
forever

no splash
from you . . .

hardly
a disturbance

you
upon the starry stream
your boat
your oars

the galaxy

through the long night (captain)

a teddy bear
commands this ship

I defer
to the calls
he makes

he tells me
to check the chart
to ensure
the stars
are where they are
supposed to be

where we
have determined
that they *need* to be

I see him
in a captain's hat

the skipper
of a boat
sailing the ocean wide

and I see him standing
calm
upon the helm . . .

gazing out
away
beyond the reach
of storms

he came from
what was *home*

companion to me
a mate

my friend

our history
is a mutual thing

he cannot steer this ship
and I
have no voice
for command

so he tells me

so
I listen

the stars
are exactly
exactly
where they
are supposed to be

we are managing
this ship
quite well

but sometimes
when he whispers
I feel . . .

I fear . . .

a small part
of me
has gone
quite crazy

the colour of the sin (is red)

the colour
of the sin
was red

I tracked it
towards the sun

the trail in the sand
was easy

there is no
subtlety
in such crime

pure . . .

I wear my purity
across my shoulders

temptation dust
fills the air
sin
enjoys an atmosphere

the closer I get
the more
my breathing
swims
in the shallows

I don't know
why
perhaps I want
to look it in the face
just once

I am
after all
as innocent
as most . . .

most
of the time

~

I don
the cape
the red lined cape

comb
my hair back
sleek
sleek

then
my cravat . . .

my *shoelace*
cravat

I breathe

this time
I breathe
deeply

it is not my sin
that is red
it is my
vision

red

I try a laugh

ha
Ha Ha HA

HA HA
HA HA

I am
the sleek
muppet vampire count

I am
the flyer
of the dark night

I am the kiss
that bites
the tongue
that licks

one
small
sweet lick

    a
    ha ha ha

the night
is mine
the moon
is mine
I am coming

and you . . .

you are mine

    a ha
    ha

the passing

he stood
mostly concealed
looking out through the curtain
and the glass

deliberately
he kept himself
in shadow

here
in the darkness
only he could watch

and here in the shadows
only he . . .

unseen

outside
was springtime

small islands —
disappearing —
of snow

the rest
was green
in the glow
of a newfound sun

and in the crystal light
she danced

free
as her arms
whirled around

free
as she spun
and kicked up
her legs

a prance
of a dance
she joined it
with everything
she had

the puff
of her breath
was a signal
sent out in smoke

he ground his teeth
behind
the curtain

watched —
avidly —
each move she made

and he wished

how wished
she had found
some other stage
on which to perform

but
there she was

there he was

and so
they stay

while the dance
goes on

the blue (above)

I
do not love
islands

the land
I was born in
was
an island

the biggest
island

it is gone now

I live on . . .

an
archipelago

I
who do not like
islands

at all

~

if I
were to hold my breath

put my head
underneath the waves

maybe
I could witness
history

there
is the street
that bifurcated
in the heart
of town

there
are the shops
that lined
the boulevard

if I float
left
at the post office tower
then
float right

if I am still able
to hold on
to my breath

still alive

that is the place
I once believed
my home was

when I raise my head
inevitably
above the salt
of this new sea
I reflect
how strange it is

to see the fishes
of the ocean deeps
at frolic
through my bedroom

and the corridor
that led
to the
once
lounge room

so far away
from home

I am . . .

we are
so very far
away
from home

~

there is no
coastline

there is no
coastline
there is no coast
no beach

just the sea
for a million
watery miles

except for me
and *this* small yard
not yet touched

not *yet*
reclaimed

I look out
and in the sea
just under the surface
I can tell
what time it is

the clockface
from the post office tower
says
three o'clock

I exhale
as the phantoms come
too near
again

~

water
rise

wash me back
inland

sun
beat down

burn me
with a baleful eye

either
I will incinerate
or
submerge

saturated

like all my world

antennae peer
above the gentle wash
of shifting waves

upper stories
stand proud
and moist

ghostly thoroughfares
swirl
beneath the tidal surface
of my mind

everything
is gone

everything
is drowned

the sky is blue
and how
I hate
that colour

dragon

what
is a dragon

I don't know

and yet
we fly

into the air
around the world

the moon

the stars

it's all
in my mind

a figment
I have
imagined

I know

I *know*

yet
here we are

    ha-a-rrr-ooo-aagh

    a-ra

come
my scaly steed
with your
super-heated breath

fly me —
red
and silver —
a circumnavigational flight
around the world

oh
the hard
of you

oh
the warm

oh
your *purr*
as we fly

your inner fire
combusting
to drive us

and so . . .

and
so . . .

take me
away
with you

take me
away

dragon 2 — across a blood red moon

is there a wind
that blows
in outer space

a breeze
to ruffle
through my hair

assuming
of course
that I have found a way
to breathe

perhaps
it is only my
imagination
playing
games with me
but . . .

I *feel* I am being
ruffled
as we fly

> *what depths*
> *within myself*
> *could conjure*
> *such a steed*
>
> *(I don't know)*

and we are
here
with a blood-red moon
before us

I wonder
can our shadow
be seen

drifting
across the scars
upon the face

a silhouette
of the long neck . . .

the long tail
of a dragon in flight

> *how deeply*
> *within myself*
> *did I go*
> *for this*

> *will there be anything*
> *left*
> *of my imagination*

flying
on a dragon's breath

two creatures
beneath
a blood-red moon

I breathe
easily
and I
feel the wind
ruffling

we *ride*

landing (like vertigo)

from this side
of the hill
looking back
and up
it was like . . .

like . . .

it was like
a thunderstorm

strobe light
followed
by the low
distant
chest-rumble
of sound

a clear sky

stars

and that strobing flash
of lightning
breaking open the night

thunder
creeping out

rolling

released
through the cracks
that the light made
in the sky

within the ground

rising
through boots

squirming the groin
before settling
in the chest

surrounding the heart
with a touch

like vertigo

and the ship
had landed

Frank Prem

the mate's shrine (a form of worship)

54

there is a stone
that came with me
from home

I kiss it
when I think
of you

flat
and smooth

a white granite
chip

a book
and a soft
brown bear

a bracelet
and a photograph

sometimes
I align them

sometimes
they are piled together
into a mound

they are like
a fingerprint

markers
of my heart
that I still
keep close

though they come
from a long
ago

I close the door
of my home

my cabin

let the dark
that lives outside
creep in

enshroud them
for awhile

images can be hard
to hold on to
when I am swimming
eternally
through the night

knowing I can touch
these few things
for a moment now and then
I feel
closer

catch (with a net)

I cast a net
out
across the waves

trying to catch
a passing thought

> *they slip*
> *and slide*

> *they escape me*

> *dark waters run*

> *ideas rise*

> *flash their silver*

> *then go down*

~

I cast my nets

draw
on the knotted cords

struggle —
hauling —
against the flow

but
should I catch
just *one* . . .

only . . .

one

heart (on the dark side) of a vacuum

my heart
is on the darker side

planting sunflowers
in an airtight room

my heart watches —
closely —
to record the moment
of first sprouting

~

my heart
lets the water
drip

so

slowly

that small piece
of soul
remaining
to the empty dead

but
can you
grow the green
my heart

when vacuum
is the state
of grace

and can you make
life
the way you did
with me

~

my heart
is taking giant-steps

to walk
is nearest kin
to fly

a little
bit of *bounce*

a little
almost-dancing

will you come home
my heart
when your green things
turn the petri dish
to brown . . .

will you blast away
from your brave failures . . .

will you try
again —
heart of mine —
or
will you leave me

waiting

an empty shell
in the state of grace
that is
a vacuum

purple hued

I used to watch
short waves
of strange rainbows
form

then run away
in hues
that seemed to me
purple

the shields were strong
then

debris repelled
and debris
burned

it is different now
since the reactor
broke

it seems energy
is not
eternal

now I see
small holes
materialize

now I watch oxygen
measured
by the flickering
of gauges

all flick-flicking
down

all
approaching a rainbow
of yellow
and of orange

of red

small dust
casts a shadow
you know

a mighty shade
across my life

each blow
to the hull
of my destiny
is an arrow
to my demise

I used to watch
in fascination
a rainbow

comprised
of purple hues

airway song

I sing no
songs

it is enough
to breathe

    h-u-u-herrr

    h-u-u-herrr

the sound
of the air
comes
just the way
I make it

in a rhythm

    h-u-u-herrr

    h-u-u-herrr

there is a temptation
here
at all times
laid out to coax my eyes
into disbelief

    h-u-u-herrr

but truly
before me
right
before me
is
forever

and I sing
if I sing
only
in the sounds
of a suited
airway

    h-u-u-herrr-way

in rhymes
of repetition

repetition

and brea-

brea-

breathing

tsh tsh

    w-h-r-r-r-r-r

    h-u-u-herrr

    h-u-u-herrr

tsh tsh

    w-h-r-r-r-r-r

the wayward

cumbulum
come here

cumbulum
come here
come here
I say

cumbulum
I know
you hear me

naughty tendril

mischievous chi . . .

CUMBULUM!
cumbulum!

oh
you test my tuntatauun

tuntatauun

cumbulum
come wrap round me

cumbulum
cumbulum
all your arms around me
child

you know
my hearts
all beat
in you

solidifying (a shadow ship)

there is a voice

      where

is a voice . . .

      there

it just began
solidifying

there is a voice
the *same* voice

where . . .

just *there*

parallel

solidifying

I
am the voice

I
am right here

they
out there
are
solidifying

I send them —
voice
and ship —
my eyes to see
my voice
solidified

reporting

> *choose starboard*
> *choose port*
> *young*
> *shadow ships*

> *report*

in voices still
solidifying

where I live

I live
at the end of days

I do not see . . .

I am on the *last*
horizon

nothing left before me
but a fall

and I live at
the end of days
I would shoot the sun
down
if I could

there is no light
shines
for me

I am in the black

living at the end of days
glory times
are behind me

a riot —
all of movement
and of sound —
pushing me to
now

I am
the end of all times
coming

the wind blows
desolation

the wind blows
desert
into my hair

blows me

one step
till I fall

accustomed (let us sing)

I whistle
the sun

whistle
for new light
rising

hum
within my breath

hold on
to hope

I make a sound
call it
song

raise my voice
to heaven

.

.

.

so
sing with me
now
is the time

sing songs of light
and of reason
lest
in the night we grow
akin
to the darkness

sing

sing out now

lest in the night
all hope
is lost
and we grow
too accustomed
to darkness

droving (the milky way)

> *hee-yah!*

> *hee-yah!*

I am herding
the stars
these
recalcitrant stars

across the wide
black plain

they are forming
a line
they are shining

> *hee-yah!*

I crack the corded whip

> *haa!*

I crack
the corded whip

> *haa! haa! haa!*

> *hee-yah!*

comet!
go
round them up

meteor!
make them line

streak . . .

you good things
streak!

go around them
get them up

    hee-yah!

star droving

    hee-yah!

the milky
way

    hee-hee-yah!

first dog

the first dog
to reach the moon
ran around
on the floor

bright light
from the orb
dark black
from the night

the first dog
to reach the moon
didn't notice the stars

wondered
if the time was ready
yet
to push the button
for a bite

first dog
to reach the moon

wasn't meant
to EVA

snuck aboard
with the astronauts

stuck his head up

    orbit boy

wagged his tail
at perigee

first dog
to reach the moon
watched the boss
step . . .

.

.

.

to the ground

    wuff wuff

support in kind
and

    hurry home

for dinner time

from eight mile plains to eight miles up

Written for the Reading Group at Eight Mile Plains State School, Queensland

I was just
a child from
the *eight mile plains*

but
I read about the stars
one day
when I was sitting
in my reading group

that
is when I knew

~

every night
I would go
outside
when the day grew dark

stand
with my head craned
up
to look at the sky

at the bright lights
and
the twinkles

that's when I knew

~

I always knew

~

yesterday
I looked down
on brisbane

trying to see
if I could spot
eight mile plains

and
I think
I can see it

there

yes
I think
it might be

there

and here am I
today

looking down

.

.

.

looking back

fishing in the mellish

I swim
like the fishes
on mellish street

they roar
and they meander
tangling up
my feet

the water
is as black
as bitumen tar

try pushing through that
you'll soon know
where you are

silver
in the light
you must come up
to breathe

mostly
air in your lungs
that will never
leave

give a wave
and make a splash
should we ever meet

I swim
with the fishes
on mellish street

at you and laughed

from the page

I draw —
by the hilt —
a length of steel

my sword

feel the weight of it

the fight
is at hand

not
just a story

~

another turn

I have read
all the way from the forge
to the battlement walls

I see
the written words
that are my opponent

and we begin
with a *clash* . . .

a brittle *claŋg*

we fight

~

chapter next

and I have taken
a lover

to know
that she is
beautiful
you need only ask
the opinion
of the king

I rest my sword . . .

a shelf
filled with bound vellum

and look
to the bed . . .

to what is written
there

to what awaits
me

~

I am riding hard —
a horse —

a well described
steed

we are *a-gallop*

we fly

the kings men
pursue

ha ha!

ha ha!

what
is written next . . .

the *penultimate*
chapter

ha ha!

they will never
take me
alive

~

where
is this place

I know nothing
of the things
that I can see

perhaps
after all
they managed
to catch me

perhaps
in the end
it was written
that I fell . . .

is this *real*

am I merely
a *fiction*

is this *now*
or
only the *final* page
of the book
that lets you read
my death

time
and again

.

.

.

the language
is sparse

perhaps obituary

the language
is dry

as dust
unto dust

but
I remember . . .

I recall
better pages

better paragraphs
where you and I
loved
and
we laughed

didn't we

Frank Prem

waiting for the day (airtight)

I breathe
from my O2 tank

I hear the air
as it hisses past
a valve

feel it
inside
my throat

a welcome stranger

~

out here
the night
is still
is black

the night
is forever

everywhere

but
I trust
in my airtight suit
I trust
in every seal and join

I trust
every god
back on earth
who made it

push the button
for a little
extra thrust

steady

I float
with the hull
beside me

this ship
is my home
my life

this ship
is my
safekeeping

and I trust
that it will stay intact
I trust it

every weld

~

faith
surrounded by the night
is a little like
old time
religion

but what else
am I to do

I have a job
just like anyone
else

and I know the night
is hungry

enough
to want to touch me

take me
hold me

keep me

~

airless

.

.

.

airtight

there is so little
that comes
in between

I believe in my ship
yes I do

I believe
in my spacesuit

and I believe
that the god
who made all my
important things
is down there

down
upon the earth
looking up

and that she loves me

she speaks
my name

and I hear her
crackle
through the radio

the voice
is in my head —
talking quietly —
again

I hear
my oxygen
flip a valve

flip a valve
right over

and I breathe

and hear her voice
telling me
that she believes
in me

making me believe
I can do
my job
in safety

and she
will be waiting

the day
that I
come down

water and crumbs

hush child
it is night time

snuggle down
while I tell a story
of what *was*

once
upon a time . . .

in a land
where the sun
shone
like honey in a jar

where
the water ran in the rills
with the joyous sound
of laughter

and the forest was alive
with creatures that walked
on their four legs
or hopped
on two

with fur
that was soft

or spikes
like a pin cushion

the birds
fanned their tails
from side to side
to admire themselves

it was there
once upon a time
a boy
went walking

he took with him
a banana
to eat as a snack
for he meant to have
a journey

so bold
he strode out
into the forest
of tall and straggly
trees
that let the sun through
for they had
only a thin canopy

and thick green
pine tree saplings
that he had to push aside
to force a path

the ground
where he walked
was littered with dead leaves
that filled the air
with eucalyptus smell
as he walked on them

but every step he took
looked the same

every direction

even the rocks
great boulders of granite
they were —
tall and brooding
and rough —
seemed alike

some of the boulders
had caves at their base

spaces
that led away
into darkness

some
had split in two
forming long and narrow
crevasses

and he was watched . . .

eyes

there were
secret eyes

watching
as he wandered
further into the forest

.

.

.

after a time
he grew weary

sat down
and peeled
and ate
his banana

wished
that he had brought
a drink

a little water

somehow
he had wandered
away
from the happy rill

the sun continued
to shine
and now
it was beating down

hot

the eyes watched him
still
but he did not know

he wondered
to himself
if
perhaps
he should go back

if he had had
enough
of journey
for the time being

but
when he turned
to look back
the way he had come
he could see
no path
only the same scrub
and forest
all around him

he heard
a thin trickling sound —
as of disturbed dirt
and skating stones —
but
saw nothing

no one

still
the eyes observed him

and he began
to walk
again

but every way
now
was the same way

every tree
was the same tree

and he wandered
and wandered

until he was
no more

~

what are you asking
child . . .

no

that is the end
of the story

well
what do *you* think
happened?

such a foolish boy
to go like that
into the forest
so unprepared

he was never heard of
again

tcha!

the eyes
were just eyes
do you think the creatures
of the forest
are unaware
of what passes?

is it *their* job
to save such a one?

child
this is not
a fairy tale

every day
is a journey
and if you are wise
you will take water . . .

yes
and leave behind you
a trail of crumbs
to find your way
home

I am the (salt) moustache

I am *fish*
my feet
both
on the ground

I swim against
the flowing
current

I swim
my head down
into the waves
as though
I am
the tide itself

the tugging
of the current

watch the cloud of sand
that swirls . . .

that I
am *stirring*
by my passage

a fish
with my legs
twisted inward
to withstand the tug

as lunar as
an ebb . . .

a wane

high tide

high tide

I wash away
the careful
cockles

I claim
as well
the sideways crab

I walk among

I tug
the sea

there is salt
now
on my moustache

cup and coven

*the cup
in my hands
is a . . .*

whiskery . . .

cat

she sang
and stirred

the dark creature
lying beside her
glanced up

*the cup
in my . . .*

~~oh~~
~~do stop~~

not words
but
thought
stated into the mind

~~make your potion~~
~~without singing me~~
~~into it~~

~~I'll wear your smelly brew~~
~~soon enough~~

she continued
in a quiet
hum
from time to time
she fetched the sheet-like
skin-like object
into the air
with her ladle

> *the cup*
> *hmm hmm*
> *hmm . . .*

yes
the *man-suit*
was ready

dried
and straightened
it could be worn

she *would* go —
escorted —
to the coven
tonight

a specialist (at *the recycled heart*)

I am
a specialist

I work at
the recycled heart

every day
I take possession
of dreams
wishes and hopes

old loves
and old lives
that have been used up

broken

it took
so much high energy
to make these things
when they were new

so much spirit
so much
desire

all of it destined
to end up
in *emotion-dumps*

eventually
packed down
smoothed over

re-scaped
and built on
but
the new buildings
the new estates would
subside
at odd times
like
anniversaries
and during *sleepless nights*

they would begin
to weep
helplessly

so I was called in
to help

I am
a *specialist*

I can take
a failed dream

a broken
and damaged
heart

put it into
the machinery of
the *re-imaginer*

that is my device
you see

I invented it
for this

so
I will melt down
the passion

the emotion

the heartbreak

to a fraction
of itself

then inject it
while it is still
hot

while it remains
malleable

make a shape
an ornament
a keepsake

a static reminder
minus the aching
and the distress

paint it
into the colour
that recalls
the best it was

then your life
can go on

you
may leave the tears
behind

leave
the disappointment
to burn away
in the *re-imaginer*

I am a specialist

I can recycle
your
broken heart

the filament song

(Inspired by Nick Harkaway's book: Gnomon)

the filament
is very fine

it slides
easily

interstitially

past the one
and around
the next

deeper
to where the electricity
fires
sending all its signals out

the filament
is very fine

will anchor there

don't be alarmed
it's only watching you

only
reading you

evaluating
you

and possibly
reporting

the filament
is very fine

is whispering to me
and I
responding

we chat a lot -
the wire
and I

and between us
we are
knowing
you

the filament
is very fine

between us
is only
what you do
what you think
what you believe you
really are

the filament is very fine

I feel that I am there

I believe
that I am there . . .

in there

I
am
with you

footsteps (and heart)

he took his
heart
to the bleeding edge

raised his head
as the sun
went down

asked the sky
to let tomorrow
come

told the stars
they could have him
now

he left
his heart
at the bleeding edge

walked away

footprints
into night

studio

(Inspired by Nick Harkaway's book: Gromon)

he fancies himself
a fisherman

as he leans
a little forward —
nearer in
to the stone —
and taps
hammer
to chisel

to rock

there

another part
of another shape
is etched in

deep enough
to show itself

deep enough
to last

he shakes chips of stone
from his smock
and leans in again
toward the next outline

the hammer strikes

the chisel bites

another chip
another line
another
etching

a med.it.a.tion

fish

fish
you be a shark
you

be a shark

he touches
fingers to a fin
to
a flank

the bitey fishy head
of it

a quickened jerk
a flip
of tail

a shaking
wilding
swinging of the head
from side to side

into the water
lapping at his feet

at the base
of a hollow
sculpting-stone

a fin
cuts through the water

distance
perspective
diminishment

nothing at all

just a fisherman

a chisel
a hammer

hollow stone
and water lapping
in a studio

Frank Prem

aquarius: where are your sheep

ganymede
ganymede

where are your sheep
gone
dear boy

was it not
you
who were the one
meant to keep them
safe from harm

yes it was

but the eagle came —
I saw —
from the stars above
to claim you

zeus is god
and you
are just a toy

a plaything
for his pleasure

for a while

~

carry water

run
his bath

carry water

bathe
his feet

fetch for him
and carry
young aquarius

but
while you drift
all around the sky
with your pitcher . . .

your pail

the sheep
that were your chore
have wandered

~

curse you
fell god

I curse you
old jove

oh
ganymede

my ganymede

your sheep
are —
all of them —
gone

Frank Prem

pisces: mailman on the piscean line

they never show
the third angle
that cuts across
from *triangulum*
through the bottom
of the square
and over to *the circlet*

it always seems easier
to join up the dots
on the left . . .

the dots on the right

to follow the line
till you get to the fish's tail

going that way it doesn't matter
which one you take
because they both end up
as a fish

but it's not like that

I always sail my ship out
to the northern fish first
up by old *andromeda b*

then cut my way past algenib
down at the bottom
of *pegasus*
with hardly a splash
in that inky sea
until I get to *the circlet*

fish head
across
to fish head

I do my stuff
and then work the tide
back along the southern line
to *al risha*

to home

yes
I get to sail both ways
in a single roundtrip
me and my ship

even the stars
need to get their mail
and some things
you can't send
like a breath
that'll carry your whistle

you just have to
go out there
by yourself
and do it

Frank Prem

capricorn: a plea to amalthea

amalthea
take this child

watch over him

help him grow

amalthea
even the great among us
need care

and if he stray —
or cause you harm —

forgive

for he will do
wondrous things

he will in turn
take care of you

and should kronos
speak the boy's name

divert him

turn the titan away

for this child
some day will surpass him

and for you . . .

I foretell
your future
is among stars

Leaving: One, Two, Three

leaving #1 blue soldier (grey)

I am
a soldier

I do not select
the battles I fight

I do not choose
among the wars

I obey
lawful orders

my uniform
is plain to see

it is plain
for everyone to see
that I am of
the un-infected brigade

I am clean
and coloured blue

sanitary
in an unclean world
I guard
the portals

don't ask me
why
don't ask
who

these are not my spheres
of knowledge

all I know
is what I have been
told
to know

and that *blue*
is the colour
of *clean*

only blue
may pass
beyond the portals
of the last ship
that I stand
before

some say
there are planets
and places
where the virus
does not thrive

and some say
that there
the blue will begin
better lives

create
un-tainted
a new blue world

only the blue

and maybe
the ships that
transport them
will all
find a way
over the years

maybe
just a few
across the long flight
to *new*

or maybe
back here
the illnesses
will die
away

and some kind of
good life
will remain

but I
am the soldier blue
and I
am in the sanitary state
of cleanliness

I obey orders
and I inspect
myself
for hints
or faint traces
or any kind of shading
of grey

the little signs
of unclean
colour

while I am blue
while ever I
am the blue
I am
a soldier

I guard
the portal

I do not choose
the battles
I fight

I guard
against signs
of grey

leaving #2 aboard

who
has the right
to say

and who
claims
to determine
my fate

false
false

I am a blue
yes
I *am*

with a touch . . .
a mere
suggestion
of dis-colour
in one discreet
corner
of this damnable suit

damnable
damnable
suit

but
who
is to say

no one can tell *me*
no one
can stop *me*

I have a place
on board

this ship —
my ship —
is the last

I am a blue
and I have
the right . . .

> *(it is no more*
> *than a hint*
>
> *a touch*
>
> *a smudging*
> *of grey*
> *that no one can see)*

my place
is to be
aboard

leaving #3 leaving (has died)

the floor of a ship
bound
into the cosmos
is neither blue
nor
is it grey

it is the floor
of the last ship
that is to leave

that
is all

a dull scuff-mark . . .

> *the structure*
> *shakes*

a dark dragged-line . . .

> *it roars*
> *and trembles*

a smear

this time the colour
is red . . .

> *the vibration*
> *of everything*

a bundle —
inert —
is the sole occupant
of a corner

ferocity unleashed
as of a storm

a suit
sprawled at all angles

mostly
of blue . . .

yes
it is the suit
of a *blue*

the violence
rises

a flower
and stem
have been drawn
in red

a ship
in the air
now

a soldier

a brave and true
guardian . . .

leaving the virus
and the planet
of home
behind

has died
in service

After Words

Author Information

Frank Prem has been a storytelling poet since his teenage years. He has been a psychiatric nurse through all of his professional career, which now exceeds forty years.

He has been published in magazines, online zines, and anthologies in Australia, and in a number of other countries, and has both performed and recorded his work as spoken word.

Frank is an Adjunct Research Associate of the School of Education, Charles Sturt University, Australia.

He lives with his wife in the beautiful township of Beechworth in North East Victoria, Australia.

Connect with Frank

Find Frank at his website www.FrankPrem.com, or through Social Media online at Facebook, X (Twitter), Instagram and YouTube.

Other Published Works

Free Verse Poetry

Small Town Kid (2018)
Devil In The Wind (2019)
The New Asylum (2019)
Herja, Devastation - With Cage Dunn (2019)
Walk Away Silver Heart (2020)
A Kiss for the Worthy (2020)
Rescue and Redemption (2020)
Pebbles to Poems (2020)
The Garden Black (2022)
A Specialist at The Recycled Heart (2022)
Ida: Searching for The Jazz Baby (2023)
From Volyn to Kherson (2023)
Alive Is What You Feel (2023)
White Whale (2024)
Pilgrim Volume 1 - Illustrated by Leanne Murphy (2024)
A Poetry Archive Volume 1 (2024)
A Poetry Archive Volume 2 (2024)
A Poetry Archive Volume 3 (2024)
A Poetry Archive Volume 4 (2024)

Picture Poetry/Spoken Image

Voices (In The Trash) (2020)
The Beechworth Bakery Bears (2021)
Sheep On The Somme (2021)
Waiting For Frank-Bear (2021)
A Lake Sambell Walk (2021)
A Few Places Near Home (2023)
The Cielonaut (2024)

What Readers Say

Small Town Kid

A modern-day minstrel. Highly recommended.
 —A. F. (Australia)

Small Town Kid is a wonderful collection.
 —S. T. (Australia)

Devil In The Wind

Trust me, this book will stay with you. Bravo!
 —K. K. (USA)

Moving, beautiful, and terrible. I was left with a profound sense of respect, as well as a reminder that we should never take for granted every precious every moment of life.
 —J. S. (South Africa)

The New Asylum

Words can't do justice to the emotional journey I travelled in (reading this collection).
 —C. D. (Australia)

If I had to pick one book over the past year that has truly resonated with me, this would be it.
 —K. B. (USA)

Walk Away Silver Heart

Instantly grips you by the throat in his step-by-step story of survival. Bravo!
 —K. K. (USA)

Outstanding!
 —B. T. (Australia)

A Kiss For The Worthy

A Celebration of Life Written in Thoughtful Bursts of Poetic Expression
—C M C (United States)

With every verse, I found myself reflecting about myself, my life, and the world.
—K

Rescue and Redemption

The passion of love in its many forms explored by one for another.
—J L (United States)

I've enjoyed every word, every breath. Every moment within the life of these stories.
—C D (Australia)

Sheep On The Somme

Museums and archivists take note~sell this in your gift shops, preserve it in your archives. Professors, teachers~share with your students.
—A R C (United States)

(This) book is a beautiful and graphic tribute to all those brave men and women who gave their lives for their countries between 1914 and 1918.
—R C (South Africa)

Ida: Searching for The Jazz Baby

I found myself deeply moved by the presentation of Ida's elusive, illusionary life.
—E G (United States)

He gives her a depth and vulnerability that the press didn't.
— A C (United Kingdom

<u>The Garden Black</u>

Prem creates verse that illuminates our world, its experiences and history.

  —S C (United Kingdom)

Prem's poetry reminds that life is fragile and fleeting ... both harsh and beautiful.

  —D G K (Canada)

<u>A Few Places Near Home</u>

The author has captured many beautiful images in this book, and is a wonderful photographer as well as a poet. This book would make a beautiful coffee table book filled with moving prose to make us ponder with gorgeous accompanying images.

  —D K (Canada)

www.FrankPrem.com